"Help! I'm taking off!" Mr Mumble tried to hold onto the drainpipe but his eyebrows had inflated like two giant kites. "Help, Fleabag," he cried, but the cat was asleep and the wind was too strong and it gusted him skywards like a feather...

An extremely funny adventure story from the author of *One Hot Penguin*.

YOUNG CORGI BOOKS

Young Corgi books are perfect when you are looking for great books to read on your own. They are full of exciting stories and entertaining pictures. There are funny books, scary books, spine-tingling stories and mysterious ones. Whatever your interests you'll find something in Young Corgi to suit you: from ponies to football, from families to ghosts. The books are written by some of the most famous and popular of today's children's authors, and by some of the best new talents, too.

Whether you read one chapter a night, or devour the whole book in one sitting, you'll love Young Corgi books. The more you read, the more you'll want to read!

Other Young Corgi books to get your teeth into

ONE HOT PENGUIN by Jamie Rix
SAMMY'S SUPER SEASON
by Lindsay Camp
ANIMAL CRACKERS by Narinder Dhami
DOG MAGIC! by Chris Priestley

MR MUMBLE'S FABULOUS FLYBROWS

MR MUMBLE'S FABULOUS FLYBROWS
A YOUNG CORGI BOOK : 0 552 547476

PRINTING HISTORY
Young Corgi edition published 2002

3 5 7 9 10 8 6 4 2

Set in 16/20pt Bembo Schoolbook
by Phoenix Typesetting, Ilkley, West Yorkshire.

Young Corgi Books are published by Transworld Publishers,
61–63 Uxbridge Road, London W5 5SA,
a division of The Random House Group Ltd,
in Australia by Random House Australia (Pty) Ltd,
20 Alfred Street, Milsons Point, Sydney, NSW 2061, Australia,
in New Zealand by Random House New Zealand Ltd,
18 Poland Road, Glenfield, Auckland 10, New Zealand
and in South Africa by Random House (Pty) Ltd,
Endulini, 5A Jubilee Road, Parktown 2193, South Africa.

Printed and bound in Great Britain by
Cox & Wyman Ltd, Reading, Berkshire

FOR ROBBIE
One day you will read this.

MR MUMBLE'S FABULOUS FLYBROWS

Jamie Rix

Illustrated by Neal Layton

Chapter One

In a grey, draughty house lived a sad, little man with his raggedy cat called Fleabag. The old man's name was

Mr Mumble and Mr Mumble hardly
ever went outside. He stayed indoors
wearing only his pyjamas, his tartan
slippers and his faded yellow dressing-
gown. There was something missing
from Mr Mumble's life. It was happiness.

The cause of his unhappiness was plain for all to see. He had the largest pair of eyebrows in the world. They jutted out on either side of his face like two window ledges. When it rained small children huddled underneath to keep dry.

They nicknamed him "Hammerhead", because he looked like a hammerhead shark.

These eyebrows were not as big as Tower Bridge, but they were bigger than a couple of Yorkshire Terriers. In hot weather they frizzed up like two threadbare sofas bursting with horsehair stuffing, but in the wet they gleamed and glistened like giant slugs.

As a child, his mother had taken him to the best doctors, but none had found a cure for excessively large eyebrows.

One had suggested that Mr Mumble should move to the Equator where the heat would make his eyebrows moult. Another had sent him to a hairdresser for a re-style, but wax, plaits and curling tongs had not made him any happier.

Mr Mumble grew up hating his eyebrows. All he ever wanted was to travel the world, but his eyebrows wouldn't let him.

Cars, taxis, boats, buses, planes and trains were just too narrow for them.

Which was why he rarely left home. Which was why, year after year after year, he sat alone in the dark, growing whiskers. Poor Mr Mumble — held prisoner by a pair of eyebrows!

Chapter Two

Then one day, while Mr Mumble was taking a shower, he heard a loud clattering outside. He quickly dried

himself, pulled on his pyjamas, dressing-gown and slippers, and opened the window. It was raining tiles. A fierce wind swirled around the chimney pot like a small tornado. Mr Mumble squeezed his eyebrows through the window and leaned out to inspect the damage to the roof, but just as he did so the storm changed direction.

"Help!" squeaked Mr Mumble as the wind filled his eyebrows and lifted his slippers off the floor.

"Help! I'm taking off!" He tried to hold onto the drainpipe but his eyebrows had inflated like two giant kites. "Help! Fleabag!" he cried, but the cat was asleep and the wind was too strong and it gusted him skywards like a feather.

He floated up through the clouds like a cork bobbing up in the sea. He shouted for help, but only a family of ducks heard his cry.

Down below, he could see London. It was tiny. The mighty River Thames snaked its way through the bustling city like a skinny earthworm. Cars clogged the roads like ants and Big Ben struck ten like the bell on a butcher's bicycle.

When Mr Mumble realized that his eyebrows had billowed out like two parachutes and he wasn't going to fall, he stopped screaming. He was flying. It was fun!

Suddenly there was a rush of cold air and a helicopter appeared by his side.

"Who gave you permission to fly?" shouted the policeman through a megaphone.

"Nobody," said Mr Mumble. "I was taking a shower when the wind got under my eyebrows and I took off!"

"Eyebrows!" gasped the policeman. "Those *things* are eyebrows?"

"When did you last see a pair of wings that were this hairy?" protested Mr Mumble.

"Never," said the policeman. "Follow me and I'll lead you down to safety."

But as the helicopter peeled off towards the ground, Mr Mumble stayed put. "Would you mind awfully if I didn't go down just yet?" he cried out. "Only I like it up here."

"But it's dangerous," yelled the policeman. "This is the sky. There are big birds up here. Not to mention big aeroplanes, big fireworks and big meteors!"

"Yes I know," smiled Mr Mumble, "but I don't get out much and this makes such a nice change."

"Flying around willy-nilly is against

the law, sir. If you don't land I could lose my job!"

"I *will* land," promised Mr Mumble, "in a moment. After I've had a bit of a fly around." The policeman sighed. "All my life I've been cooped up by these monstrous

eyebrows, and now that I've discovered what they're for, I want to fly them!"

To prove his point, Mr Mumble swooped, looped and double-hooped over a supermarket car park to admiring "ooh's" and "aah's" from astonished shoppers.

"Is it a bird?" they exclaimed.

"Is it a plane?"

"No. It's a man with incredibly large eyebrows!"

"*Fly*brows, if you please!" laughed Mr Mumble. "From now on these hairy monsters are called flybrows!"

And with that he soared into the sun like a hero.

"Ready to go home now?" asked the copper in the chopper.

"Oh yes," chuckled Mr Mumble. "That's quite enough flying for one day. I shall come up tomorrow and have another flit around!"

"Hmmm, we'll have to see about that!" muttered the policeman. "Now, is everything set for landing?"

"How should I know?" said Mr Mumble. "I've never flown before. Do I look set?"

Just then a strong wind surged from the west and whipped him up through the clouds.

"Where are you going?" shouted the policeman.

"I don't know," wailed the old man. "My flybrows are out of control!"

Chapter Three

There was a problem. Mr Mumble was flying over the Channel heading for France, but didn't know how to land his

flybrows. Somebody needed to get him
down before there was an accident.

The Royal Air Force was called in to
co-ordinate the rescue. Wing
Commander Plank was in charge.

"We'll catch him over Paris," he
announced.

"Yes, but how does one land
flybrows?" asked his second-in-
command.

"I have a plan," smirked the Wing Commander, "to cut the flybrows down to size! Find me a beautician."

A beautician was found, attached to the end of a rope and hoisted into the air over Paris. Mr Mumble had just had an eyeful of the Eiffel Tower when this beautiful lady appeared by his side.

"Have you come to save me?" he asked. "I've got a cat called Fleabag at home who needs feeding."

"Hold still," said the French beautician, flashing a pair of silver tweezers. "I shall be plucking your flybrows with my tweezers until there is no more hair in them and you fall to the ground."

Mr Mumble thought it was a splendid idea, but the tweezers were far too small for the job and they snapped.

"Bally blast!" cursed the Wing Commander when he heard that the beautician had failed. "We need something stronger than tweezers to clip his wings!" Meanwhile, Mr Mumble floated on over Europe. "Get me the Turkish Ambassador on the phone."

Mr Mumble was starting to panic. He'd been flying for hours. He'd seen a bobsleigh run in Obergurgl, a bullfight

in Barcelona, and a gondolier in Venice. What if nobody could trim his flybrows? He'd be up there for ever!

But not if the Turkish Ambassador had his way. It is a well-known fact that turkey pluckers have the strongest fingers

in the world, from plucking feathers out of turkeys, and that Turkey has the strongest turkey pluckers in the world!

When a Turkish turkey plucker dropped through the clouds on a harness and started plucking Mr Mumble's flybrows, the old man was sure that he'd been saved.

But his flybrows were super-huge and super-tough. They would not be plucked. In fact the turkey plucker sprained his wrist and had to retire hurt.

"Help!" wailed Mr Mumble as he glided over the Sphinx. "I want to go home!" But he couldn't. Over the Taj Mahal he flew, over the Great Wall

of China and Mount Everest, where a couple of brave Sherpas tried to catch him in the world's largest butterfly net.

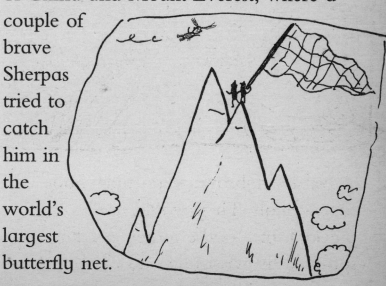

Unfortunately they caught a Malaysian jumbo jet by mistake and had to walk home from Kuala Lumpur.

Chapter Four

Mr Mumble was chasing kangaroos in the Australian outback, when the Wing Commander came up with his third idea. "Get me the Flying Barber!" he

bawled, and the Flying Barber was duly got. He attempted to shave Mr Mumble's flybrows whilst dangling in mid-air, but the flybrows blunted the clippers.

Mr Mumble flew on.

A topiarist was scrambled in Japan. She left her bonsai trees mid prune and took off on a flying trapeze with a hedge trimmer in her hand. But the flybrows were too thick and the hedge trimmer jammed.

Mr Mumble flew on.

In Argentina a gardener was called in from his polo fields and sent up into the sky with a lawnmower.

But Mr Mumble's flybrows were so gigantic that the gardener had barely made a start on the cutting before his lawnmower ran out of petrol.

Mr Mumble flew on.

"This is our last throw of the dice," admitted the Wing Commander. "The wind is steering Mr Mumble towards Canada. When he arrives we must unleash our secret weapon."

"Which is?" asked his wide-eyed assistant.

"Lumberjacks!" roared the Wing Commander.

"Lumberjacks!" squeaked the startled assistant.

"With chainsaws!"

"With *chainsaws*?" The second-in-command noticed a mad glint in his boss's eye.

"I'll trim those flybrows," snarled Wing Commander Plank, "if it's the last thing I do!"

Chapter Five

Mr Mumble got the shock of his life when fifteen helicopters suddenly appeared over the Rocky Mountains.

Hanging underneath each helicopter in a circular steel cage was a large lumberjack with a chainsaw.

"What are you going to do?" trembled Mr Mumble.

"We're going to trash the flybrows," said the lumberjacks.

"Close your eyes. We'll be through before you know it."

"I hope so," said Mr Mumble. "I'm only wearing pyjamas and it's rather cold flying around the world. And

my cat still hasn't been fed."

As the helicopters swung the cages into position, the lumberjacks started their chainsaws with an ear-splitting roar. Then they launched their attack on the flybrows while Mr Mumble closed his eyes.

When he opened them again, the chainsaws were broken and his flybrows were as big and bushy as ever. Not one single hair had been touched.

"Wow!" said the lumberjacks. "Them flybrows is tougher than trees!"

"So what's going to happen to me now?" asked the old man.

"You're going to have to fly around the world for ever," came the reply. "Nobody knows how to get you down."

Poor Mr Mumble. He was so unhappy. He'd never see Fleabag again. A tear rolled down his wrinkled face as a fresh wind blew in from the north and nudged him back across the Atlantic Ocean towards England.

Chapter Six

Halfway across the water, Mr Mumble met a family of ducks. He recognized them as the same family of ducks he'd seen flying over his roof when he first took off. The littlest duckling had fallen behind his bigger brothers and sisters. His mother was keeping him awake and urging him to fly by nudging him with her bill. The family was obviously tired and the mother feared that her baby would not make it to dry land.

Mr Mumble realized that he was the duckling's only hope. He flew alongside the father and raised his flybrows as if to say, "There's room on top if you need it." The offer was gratefully received and the parents shepherded their children onto the top of the flybrows to rest. The little one fell asleep instantly.

After an hour or so, Mr Mumble noticed that something strange was happening. Either the clouds were rising or he was sinking. He checked his position against the horizon and realized that it was *him*. It was definitely him! The weight of the ducks on his flybrows was ever so slowly pushing him down to earth. Mr Mumble let out a shriek of glee. He needed more birds!

He stopped everything that flew past – seagulls, swallows, housemartins, geese – and urged them to jump on. A lost

 puffin, a flock of flamingos, six skuas and a kittyhawk all settled down for a snooze and a chat. And with every bird that took advantage of the flybrow "rest zone", Mr Mumble edged closer and closer to the earth.

By the time his house came into view he was only a few metres above the chimney pots. His heart skipped a beat. "Whatever you do, don't jump off now!" he warned the resting birds. "Flying the nest is forbidden until my feet are firmly back on the ground. I do not want to take off again!" Flying around the world once was more than enough for Mr Mumble. But even as he spoke he saw a sight that made his blood run cold.

It was a hungry-looking Fleabag clinging to the chimney pot.

It didn't take Mr Mumble long to work out what was going to happen next. After all, Fleabag was a cat and the birds were birds.

Chapter Seven

Hissing, spitting and fully clawed, Fleabag sprang from the chimney pot and landed on top of the flybrows. There was a flurry of excitement as the squawking birds leapt to their feet, flapped their wings and fluttered away, leaving Fleabag standing all alone in the middle.

With less weight on top Mr Mumble slowly started to rise again. He tried to grab hold of the roof, but he missed. He was helpless with rage as his house and home slowly disappeared from view.

Fleabag didn't say a word. He hid his face behind his paw and pretended he wasn't there.

"Now what are we going to do?" asked the old man, coldly.

I don't know why you're so grumpy, thought the cat. You always said you wanted to see the world. Now you can see it twice! He miaowed plaintively. Fleabag was hungry.

"We're just going to have to wait until we can find some more birds," said Mr Mumble. "And next time, Fleabag, please don't try to eat them!"

Fortunately they did not have to wait long, because just then the biggest bird in the world appeared through the clouds. It was the copper in his chopper.

"You're not still flying, are you?" he said.

"Been round the world," said Mr Mumble. "And it looks like I might be going back again if you don't find something heavy to weigh down my flybrows."

The policeman took the hint, but the helicopter was too big and the blades too dangerous to land on the flybrows.

So he made a beeline for the farm directly below and picked up the first heavy thing he could find.

"Will this do?" he asked a bit later, opening the door to his helicopter to show off his prize.

"Perfect," smiled Mr Mumble. "Load 'em up!"

And that was why, half an hour later, when Mr Mumble finally landed on the roof of his house, he had thirty little piglets sleeping soundly on his flybrows. That all took place a few years ago. Nowadays a happy Mr Mumble and his Thirty Sleepy Pigs are fabulously famous. They fly to air shows all round the world and give demonstrations to prove that pigs *can* fly, so long as there's a pair of flybrows to sleep on, of course!

THE END

ABOUT THE AUTHOR

Jamie Rix originally started writing and producing comedy for TV and radio, including such programmes as *Alas Smith and Jones*, starring Mel Smith and Griff Rhys Jones, and *Radio Active*. Jamie's first children's book, *Grizzly Tales for Gruesome Kids*, was published in 1990 and won the Smarties Prize Children's Choice Award. Since then he has written children's books for a wide variety of age groups, including *Johnny Casanova – the Unstoppable Sex Machine*, for older readers, and several sequels to the *Grizzly Tales* . . . This book and its sequels have been adapted into an award-winning television animation series.

Jamie's first book for Young Corgi was the very funny *One Hot Penguin*, which *The Times Educational Supplement* called 'an excellent book with a double-edged resolution'. His latest project is THE WAR DIARIES OF ALISTAIR FURY – the hilarious account of an eleven-year-old boy desperate for revenge on his older brother and sister. *Bugs on the Brain*, the first book in the series, is being published by Corgi Yearling Books in May 2002.

Jamie is married with two grown-up sons and he lives in London.

ONE HOT PENGUIN
Jamie Rix

Whistler is one hot penguin!

All over town, it's boiling hot. At the
zoo, the animals are dying for some
ice-cream. The warthogs are wilting,
the parrots are parched and the snakes
are sweating. And sitting beside a
dried-up pool is a very hot penguin
called Whistler!

Then along comes Phelan Whelan — a
small boy with a big anorak, despite
the weather. Whistler spots his chance
for escape. He dives into Phelan's
pocket and sets off on the first stage
of his journey to the South Pole!

A fishy tale from a very funny author.

Young Corgi books are perfect for
building reading confidence.

0 552 547379